MAR 1 1

# Too Many Fairies

## A Celtic Tale

Retold by
**Margaret Read MacDonald**

Illustrated by
**Susan Mitchell**

Marshall Cavendish Children

For Matilda, who just arrived.
I hope you enjoy our earth.
May you LOVE IT! LOVE IT!
LOVE IT!
— Granny Mac

For my dear nieces, Sadie
and Holly
—S.M.

My retelling of "Too Many Fairies" is derived from a tale told in both Scotland and Ireland. For other versions, see Barbara Ker Wilson's *Scottish Folk-Tales and Legends* (Oxford: Oxford University Press, 1954) and *Folktales for Reading and Telling* by Leila Berg and George Him (New York: World Publishing, 1966). In folktale indexes, see Motif F381.8 Spinning fairies lured away from house by fire alarm. Joseph Jacob's *Celtic Folk and Fairy Tales* (New York: G.P. Putnam, 1954) has a darker Irish version of the story set in Tipperary. For suggestions about telling this story, see *Shake-it-up Tales* by Margaret Read MacDonald (Little Rock: August House, 2000, p.122).     — M.R.M.

Text copyright © 2010 by Margaret Read MacDonald
Illustrations copyright © 2010 by Susan Mitchell
All rights reserved
Marshall Cavendish Corporation
99 White Plains Road
Tarrytown, NY 10591
www.marshallcavendish.us/kids

The illustrations are rendered in watercolor.
Book design by Vera Soki
Editor: Margery Cuyler

Printed in Malaysia (T)
First edition
1 3 5 6 4 2

LIBRARY OF CONGRESS CATALOGING-IN-PUBLICATION DATA

MacDonald, Margaret Read, 1940-
 Too many fairies : a Celtic Tale / by Margaret Read MacDonald;
illustrated by Susan Mitchell. — 1st ed.
  p. cm.
 Summary: An old woman complains about all the housework
she has to do, but when some fairies come to help her she finds
that they are more trouble than they are worth.
 ISBN 978-0-7614-5604-9
[1. Folklore—Ireland.] I. Mitchell, Susan, 1962- ill. II. Title.
PZ8.1.M15924To 2010
398.209415—dc22
[[E]] 2009007128

There was once an old woman who hated housework! Wash the dishes! Sweep the floor! Make the bed! Do the knitting.
One day she began to grumble.
"Work! Work! Work!
How I hate it! Hate it! Hate it!"
No sooner were these words out of her mouth than there came a knocking at the door . . .

Knock! Knock! Knock!

"Your luck has come! Open the door!
Let me in and you'll work no more!"
The little old woman opened the door . . .
and in rushed a little fairy.

The fairy raced to the sink and began
to clatter and bang away at the dishes.

clankety     clankety
       clankety                clankety

"Well, if she is going to do the dishes, I will sweep the floor," said the old woman.
But still she grumbled.
"Work! Work! Work!
How I hate it! Hate it! Hate it!"
And right away she heard,

Knock! Knock! Knock!

"Your luck has come! Open the door!
Let me in and you'll work no more!"

Another fairy ran in, snatched up the broom,
and began to sweep dust all over the house!

*swishety* *swishety* *swishety*
*swishety* *swishety*
*swishety*

"Well, then I will make the bed," said the old
woman. But soon she was grumbling again.
"Work! Work! Work!
How I hate it! Hate it! Hate it!"

Knock! Knock!
Knock!

"Your luck has come! Open the door!
Let me in and you'll work no more!"
A third fairy rushed in and began to
shake the bedclothes.

flumpety    flumpety    flumpety

"Then I will work on my knitting," said the old woman.

clickety   clickety   clickety

"Work! Work! Work!
How I hate it! Hate it! Hate it!"
but then . . .

Knock!   Knock!
Knock!

"Your luck has come! Open the door!
Let me in and you'll work no more!"
In rushed ANOTHER fairy and snatched up
the knitting.

clankety clankety
clankety

swishety swishety
swishety

flumpety flumpety flumpety

clickety clickety clickety

The old woman was surrounded by rackety fairies.
"These fairies are driving me crazy!" she yelled.

"Fairies STOP!"

And suddenly they stopped.

The house was quiet.
The bed was made, the floor was swept,
the dishes were done, the knitting was finished.
"Thank you, fairies," but before the old woman
could finish thanking them . . .
the fairies began to tear everything apart again!

They ripped up the bedcovers,

dirtied the floor,

tore up the knitting,

and smeared up the dishes.

Then . . . they began all over again!

clankety clankety
clankety

swishety swishety
swishety

flumpety flumpety flumpety

clickety clickety clickety

"They will never LEAVE!" shouted the
old woman. "TOO MANY FAIRIES!"

She rushed to the village wise woman.
"My house is overrun with fairies! They won't
stop working!"
"Oh my," said the Wise Woman. "They've come
to *help*. You haven't been *complaining*, have you?"
"Well maybe . . . at first."
"Oh, no! You'll never be rid of them!"

"Well, here is what you must try. Stand
outside your door and shout, 'Fairies come
quick! Fairies come quick!' The fairies will
run out to see what is happening. You must
jump back inside the house and lock the
door! Then, quickly . . . turn everything all
topsy-turvy . . . broom . . . dishes . . .
bedcovers . . . knitting . . .
Do NOT open the door!
And never complain again!"

The little old woman did just as she was told.
"Fairies come quick! Fairies come quick!"
"What!" The fairies rushed out to see what
was happening.

The little old woman ran inside and bolted the door.
She stood the broom upside down in the corner.
She put the dishes upside down in the sink.
She tied the bedcovers in knots.
She pulled apart the knitting and shoved the needles
into her yarn.

The fairies were banging on the door.
"Your luck has come! Open the door!
Let us in and you'll work no more!"

The old woman kept very quiet.
The old woman did not move.

The fairies stirred around and fussed.

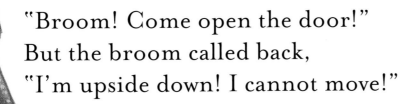

"Broom! Come open the door!"
But the broom called back,
"I'm upside down! I cannot move!"

"Dishes! Come let us in!"
"We're upside down in the
sink. We cannot come."

"Knitting needles! Come
open the door!"
"We're stuck in the yarn;
we cannot get out!"

"Bedcovers! Get up and
come open this door!"
"We're all tangled up.
We cannot move."

Those fairies began to grumble and growl.
"Then your luck is GONE!
We'll work no MORE!"

And they stomped away to their fairy hill.

At last all was quiet.
The old woman washed her dishes.
She swept her floor. She made her bed.
Then she sat down and began to do
her knitting.
But soon . . .

"Work! Work! Work! How I . . ."
She stopped just in time.
"How I . . . love it!
Love it! LOVE IT!"